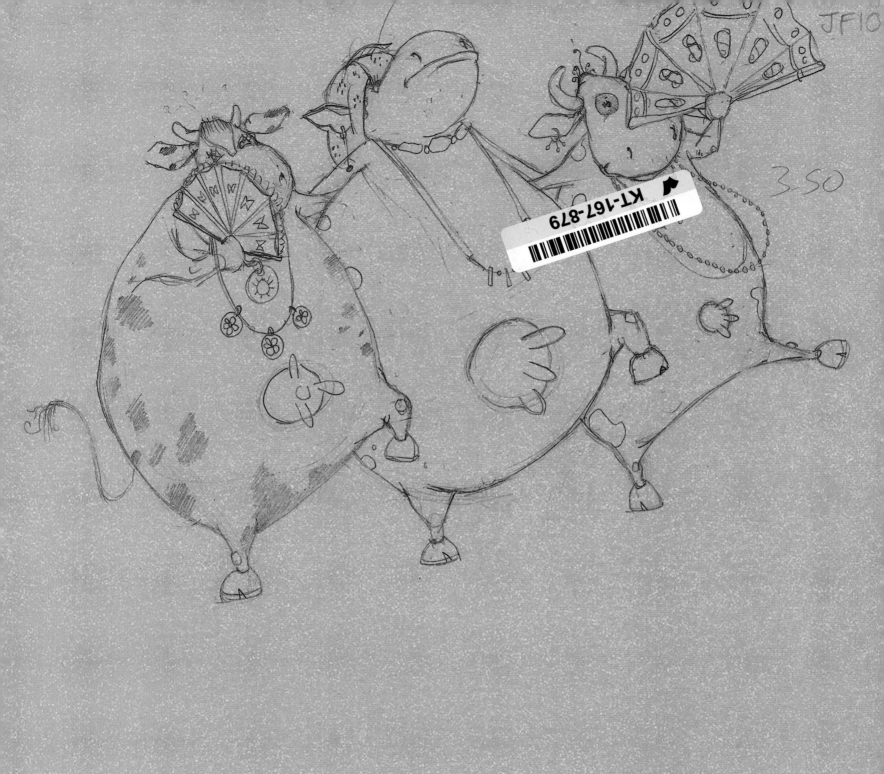

3.50

© Siphano Picture Books, 2003 for the text and illustrations

First published in the United Kingdom in 2003 by Siphano Picture Books Ltd.,
Regent's Place, 338 Euston Road, London NW1 3BT

www.siphano.com

British Library Cataloguing-in-Publication Data
A catalogue record for this book is available from the British Library

Printed in the EU

ISBN: 1-903078-64-4
1-903078-65-2 (PB)

THE BESPECTACLED DOG

and Singers of Rachel's Farm

written by *EMILY HORN*

illustrated by *URSULA BUCHER*

SIPHANO PICTURE BOOKS

FARMER RACHEL had
a lot of things to take to town:
cakes to sell at the market,
books to return to the library,
her father's suit to drop off at
the cleaner's, and one or two
other things.

It was hard fitting
everything into the car, and
somehow she forgot to load one
of the baskets into the back.

As Rachel drove off,
Ralph the Dog saw the basket
sitting in the driveway. He barked
and chased after her, but she thought
he was just saying goodbye, and didn't
bother to stop.

Meanwhile, the Hen Sisters had discovered
the basket, and were curiously looking inside.
What a find! It was full of old clothes to go to
the school jumble sale.

On top were two old straw hats – one for each of them.
The hats had lost some of their shape, but the Hen Sisters
thought they were most becoming!

They admired their reflections
in the duck pond, then went to show off
their hats to everyone on the farm. They
waddled and swayed along, and were perfectly
charming to everyone they met.

"Good day, Miss Duck... Mr Pig..."
"Lovely day, Ms Goose, isn't it?"

Soon the Cows heard about
the hats, and they rushed to look
in the basket too.

Nothing was quite their size,
but they found some nice jewellery –
earrings, necklaces, two large fans and
a lace scarf. They shared everything
between them, then stood on tiptoe
to admire their reflections in the
window. How beautiful they looked!

The Cows decided to go for a stroll,
to meet their friends and acquaintances.
They walked along taking small, elegant
steps, smiling and winking.

"Good day, Mr Hare... Mrs Otter..."
"Bright day today, Miss Squirrel,
isn't it?"

All this made Ralph the Dog curious. Was there something in the basket for him?

He found a Hawaiian shirt that fitted perfectly, and an old pair of spectacles.

Ralph looked at himself in the mirror of the farm truck... Extraordinary! What a dog!

He wanted to show off his new outfit, so he decided to drive into the village (after all, he was the only animal in the farm with a driving licence...)

As soon as Ralph started up the engine, the Hen Sisters ran over. "Please take us with you!" they begged. So Ralph let them sit in the passenger's seat.

As they drove down the road,
they met the Cows, who wanted
to come along too. They had to
sit in the back, but they were
so worn out from walking that
they didn't mind.

As they drove into
town, Ralph sang
his favourite song,
while the Hen Sisters
sang the chorus and
the Cows stomped
and clapped.

They drove past
the Town Hall and
the marketplace,
waving at everybody.

When they reached
the village school,
there was Rachel.
She was apologising
to the schoolteacher
for forgetting the
basket of clothes for
the school jumble
sale.

"Hello, Rachel..." said Ralph the Dog.
"Good morning, Miss!" cried
the Hen Sisters.
"Nice day, isn't it?" said
the Cows.

Rachel couldn't believe her eyes... Those were *her* cows and *her* hens and *her* dog sitting in *her* truck, wearing *her* old clothes which were supposed to be going to the jumble sale!

"Take off those clothes and go back to the farm at once!" she said. "Those clothes are for the school jumble sale!"

"NO!" barked Ralph the Dog.

"NO!" clacked the Hen Sisters.

"NOOOO!" mooed the Cows...

Rachel was upset.
"HOW CAN YOU BE SO SELFISH?
The schoolchildren are counting on the jumble
sale to raise money for their new library."

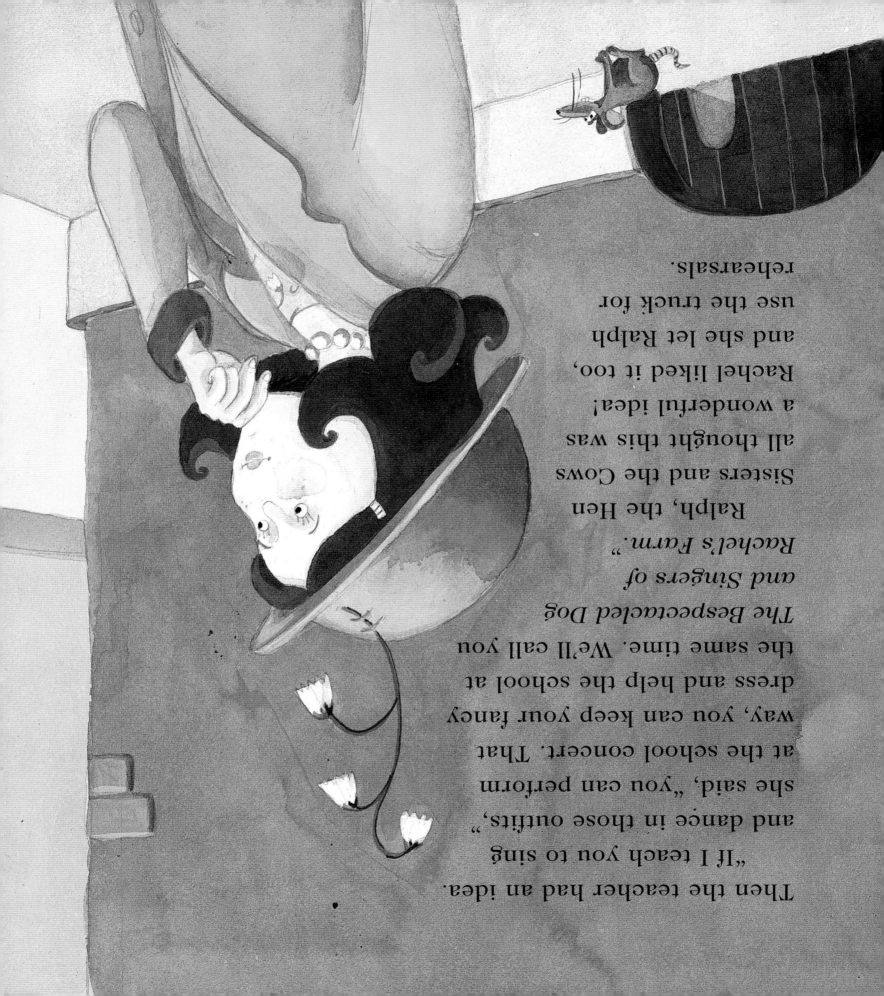

Then the teacher had an idea.
"If I teach you to sing
and dance in those outfits,"
she said, "you can perform
at the school concert. That
way, you can keep your fancy
dress and help the school at
the same time. We'll call you
*The Bespectacled Dog
and Singers of
Rachel's Farm.*"

Ralph, the Hen
Sisters and the Cows
all thought this was
a wonderful idea!
Rachel liked it too,
and she let Ralph
use the truck for
rehearsals.

So each day, when they had finished their work on the farm, Ralph drove the Hen Sisters and the Cows to the school. They wore their fancy dress and the school teacher taught them to sing and dance. It was hard work, but they enjoyed it.

Before the day of the school concert, the teacher posted large signs around the village:

THIS YEAR'S SCHOOL CONCERT – MUSIC AND DANCE BY THE BESPECTACLED DOG AND SINGERS OF RACHEL'S FARM.

People came from far and wide to see them, and everyone loved the show! There was lots of applause and the animals gave several encores.

After that, Rachel let all her farm animals stroll in the village after work. Ralph the dog, the Hen Sisters and the Cows were now famous, and everybody rushed to say hello.

After that, things soon got back to normal on Rachel's farm. Ralph the dog, the Hen Sisters and the Cows went back happily to full-time work on the farm.

As for those old clothes, the animals keep them safely hidden in the barn – for the next fund-raising show!